This is an Oggly

With their hearing horns, they can hear ants cough and earthworms burp.

Ogglies sleep when they feel like it, day or night.

Oggly hair is so hard that it can't be cut, even with the sharpest scissors.

Their lumpy noses adore the smelliest stenches.

Oggly teeth can crack anything: glass, iron, plastic, wood, and stone.

Oggly muscles are very strong and as tough as steel.

Oggly stomachs can digest anything. Ogglies never get tummy ache.

They like to bathe in mud and muck.

STARFISH BAY
CHILDREN'S BOOKS

An Imprint of Starfish Bay Publishing Pty Ltd
www.starfishbaypublishing.com

THE OGGLIES: A DRAGON PARTY FOR FIREBOTTOM

First North American edition Published by Starfish Bay Children's Books in 2016
ISBN: 978-1-76036-025-2
Die Olchis – Ein Drachenfest für Feuerstuhl © Verlag Friedrich Oetinger, Hamburg 2010
Published by agreement with Verlag Friedrich Oetinger
Translated by David-Henry Wilson
Printed and bound in China by Beijing Zhongke Printing Co., Ltd
Building 101, Songzhuang Industry Zone, Beijing 101118

Erhard Dietl, born 1953 in Regensburg, studied at the Academy of Graphic Arts and the Academy of Fine Arts in Munich. He is an author, illustrator, and songwriter. He has written over 100 books, available in translation in numerous languages around the world. Erhard Dietl has been awarded the Austrian Youth Literature Prize, and other notable literary awards.

Also by Erhard Dietl

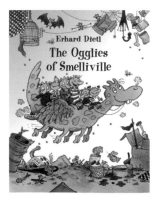

Erhard Dietl

The Ogglies
A Dragon Party
for Firebottom

⭐ STARFISH BAY
CHILDREN'S BOOKS

The green Ogglies are hard at work on the trash dump in Smelliville.
Oggly-Dad is knocking together a gadget for mud-throwing.
Oggly-Mom is feeding Oggly-Baby with some wonderfully stinky fish bones.
Oggly-Grandma is sewing a trash bag carpet for the Oggly cave. And Oggly-Grandpa is training his big, fat toads. They're supposed to be learning how to walk a tightrope.

The Oggly twins would like to go on an outing with Firebottom. But something's wrong. Firebottom is lying all miserable and motionless in front of his garage. His nose feels cold, and there's not a single cloud of smoke coming out of his nostrils.
The Oggly twins are worried. "Slimy sludge and cheesefeet! What's the matter with Firebottom?"

"Why are you so sad, Firebotty?" asks one twin with great concern.
"What can we do?" sighs the other Oggly twin. "We need to make him better!"
"I think I know what he needs," says Oggly-Mom.
She fetches a bucket full of oozy brown mess and rubs it all over Firebottom.
"Maybe he's just got cold feet?" suggests Oggly-Grandma.
She puts six thick, warm, stinky socks on the dragon's feet.
"He's hungry, that's what it is!" shouts Oggly-Dad.
He sticks a pot full of yucky, mucky poop soup under Firebottom's nose.

Oggly-Grandpa says, "Maybe a nice poem would cheer him up."
So he stands right beside Firebottom and recites,
"High in the sky dragons should fly,
Never sulk and never sigh.
Fruity stinks in a ponky pot,
He who's happy laughs a lot."

But nothing has the slightest effect. Firebottom just
continues to gaze sadly out of the dirty washing, and
doesn't let out even so much as a burp.

"I think I know what's wrong with him," cries one of the Oggly twins.
"Firebottom's got noone to play with. He needs a few dragon friends."
"Of course, that's what it is," says Oggly-Mom. "I've got a positively poopy idea.
Let's invite a few dragons around to celebrate his birthday. What do you think?"
"Cheesefeet and sludgy slime!" cry the Ogglies. "We'll give him a real live
Oggly party!"
You should know that Ogglies celebrate their birthday
whenever they feel like it and as often as they want.
Until now, they've never celebrated Firebottom's
birthday.

Straightaway, they start preparing for the party.
The Oggly twins and Oggly-Grandpa decorate Firebottom's
garage, and Oggly-Grandma lays the beautiful new trash bag
carpet out in front. Oggly-Mom bakes a gigantic stinky cake and
boils a few pots of yucky, mucky poop soup.
"Look!" she cries. "Firebottom is happy! His nose is starting to
smoke again!"

"Firebottom should have a really nice birthday present,"
says Oggly-Grandpa.
And since Oggly-Dad is such a D-I-Y expert, he sets to work immediately.
He makes a great big Oggly cuddly toy.
Everything he needs is here on the trash dump.

The Oggly twins bring Batty the bat out of his cage.
His job is to fly around inviting guests to the birthday party.
Batty knows practically every dragon in the neighborhood.
"Get a move on!" cry the Oggly twins. "Put your foot on the gas, mind
you don't crash, full speed ahead, and back in a flash!"

In no time, Batty is back again.
He's brought Rocky Red with him. Rocky Red is a great
fire-spitter— when he opens his mouth, hot flames come
darting out.

Firebottom is pleased to see Rocky Red and puffs a few
small clouds of stinky smoke out of his nostrils.

Rocky Red has brought him a present: a gigantic whoopee cushion. Firebottom is delighted. He's always wanted one of those.

The next to arrive at the trash dump is Blinky Blue. As Blinky is very short-sighted, he wears a large pair of dragon spectacles.

His hair is beautifully cut and combed, and today he's put on some extra shiny shoes. Blinky Blue is a very neat and tidy dragon.

He has also brought a present: home-baked dragon-yum-yums of mashed maggot and sliced slug.
Firebottom is delighted. He could eat dragon-yum-yums all day long.

The last to arrive is Leah Fang, a Chinese girl dragon. On her head she is wearing a long and elegant snake. She greets Firebottom with a nice, hot dragon kiss full on the nose, which immediately makes his cold nose a bit warmer and his cheeks a bit redder.
Leah Fang has also brought a present: a bag of Chinese rockets and firecrackers.
Firebottom is delighted. Now they'll have a great fireworks display.

Fish bones stinky, bottoms smelly,
Could you have a finer party?
Fiery flames are spitting, springing!
Listen to the ding-dongs dinging!
Insects big and insects small
dance and prance and have a ball.
Rats and frogs look really cute
playing nice tunes on the flute.

Dragons grunt, and Ogglies cackle,
rockets soar, and fireworks crackle.
Oggly stinks are everywhere,
and fruity reeks rip through the air.
Pots of mucky poop soup bubble.
Oggly-Mom took lots of trouble,
and her food tastes really yummy –
a treat for every Oggly tummy.

The Oggly twins have learned to play
some Oggly games on such a day:
throwing rubber tires is fun,
though there's a puncture in this one.
Firebottom's caught four tires somehow,
and there's a fifth one coming now.

Next up is a dragon race,
but who can match Firebottom's pace?

The dragons zoom across the skies,
chasing midges, gnats and flies.

And who do you think takes first position
in the diving competition?

All too soon night falls, and Rocky Red and Blinky Blue have to go home.
"We'll come again soon!" they call out to Firebottom. "It's been a great party!"
But the Chinese girl dragon doesn't want to go.
"Maybe Leah Fang can spend the night here," suggests one of the Oggly twins.
Leah Fang and Firebottom breathe out a few enthusiastic clouds of smoke.
"That sounds like a good idea to me," says Oggly-Dad

.

And so Oggly-Dad has to do some more D-I-Y. This time, he gets Oggly-Grandpa to help him build an extension to Firebottom's garage. This will make an Oggly guest-house for Firebottom's friends. Leah Fang is the first guest to sleep there.

"We handled that really well," says Oggly-Dad.
"Firebottom looks very pleased with life."
Oggly-Mom is already lying in her box.
"Now it's time for all of us to go to bed," says
Oggly-Dad.
"All you stinkerlings, good night.
Close your eyes now and sleep tight.
Slithery sludge and cheesy feet,
life is sweaty-armpit sweet!"

Birthday Song for Firebottom

Frogs are here to croak and croon.
Rats are whistling the tune.
Fleas are jumping here and there,
spiders swinging everywhere.

Firebot is quite delighted,
laughs a lot, and gets excited.
Everybody's full of joy,
especially the birthday boy!

Ogglies never wash or brush their teeth.

Ogglies hate all the foods we like.

They relish trash, and they love anything rotten or moldy.

They enjoy muck soup with fishbones, shoe-sole schnitzel, and stinky cake.

They love anything with a steamy, stinky stench.

They find the scent of perfume absolutely disgusting.

Ogglies are strong. They can throw a rubber tire sixty feet.

They like to jump around in sludgy puddles of mud.

Even flies faint at the reek of their bad breath.

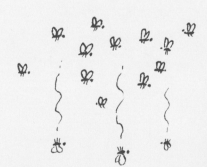

Dragon Firebottom is the Ogglies' pet. They can fly all over the place on his back.